Barney's Song

I love you, you love me
We're a happy family!
With a great big hug,
And a kiss from
Me to You!
Won't you say
You love me too?

Contents

Published by Pedigree Books Limited
Beech Hill House, Walnut Gardens, Exeter, Devon EX4 4DH.
E-mail books@pedigreegroup.co.uk
Published 2004

Pedigree®

£7.99

Meet My Friends

Barney

Hello friends! I'm so glad that you could join me in my super-dee-duper new annual! Baby Bop, BJ and all our friends have been having so much fun using their imaginations. There are so many things to discover and learn about! This year, I met lots of new friends at the zoo. Inside, you can see pictures of all the animals we met there. Hope to see you very soon!

BJ

Hi everyone! My name is BJ. I love running, jumping and riding my scooter. Oh, and I like football, baseball - in fact, I love all sports, they're so much fun! Especially when I play them with Barney and my sister Baby Bop.

Baby Bop

Well hello, everybody! My name is Baby Bop and I'm one of Barney's very best friends. I am three year's old and I just love dressing up and playing make-believe. I really like singing, dancing, painting and making things, but my favourite thing in the world is my Blankey!

Barney's
Many Hats!

WHAT CAN BARNEY BE?

Land ahoy!
My ship takes you across the ocean.

**What can Barney be?
Circle what Barney needs to
do his job.**

9

Good morning!
I grow the food you like to eat.

It may be too big, or it may be too little.
It might even have a hole in the middle.

What can Barney be?
Circle what Barney needs to
do his job.

And it might be coloured red, blue, or green.

I'm always ready to come to the rescue!
Call me and I'll jump on my truck.

What can Barney be?
Circle what Barney needs to
do his job.

13

Come on in!
I clean, feed, and watch over my animal friends.

14

And if someone saw my silly hat, they'd .
think it was the funniest thing they'd seen.

**What can Barney be?
Circle what Barney needs to
do his job.**

And I like it because it feels like part of me!

Are you lost? Is there trouble?
Just call me and I'll come to help you.

**What can Barney be?
Circle what Barney needs to
do his job.**

17

OLD MACDONALD HAD A FARM

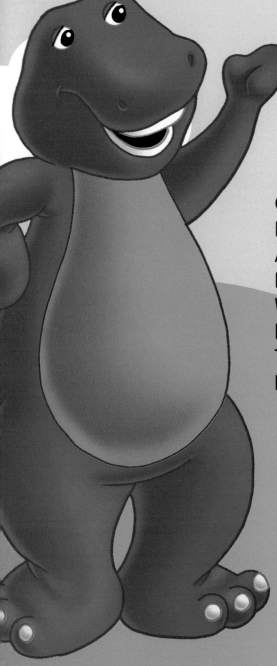

Old Macdonald had a farm
EIEIO
And on this farm he had some cows
EIEIO
With a moo, moo, here and moo, moo, there
Here a moo
There a moo
Everywhere a moo,moo

Old Macdonald had a farm
EIEIO
And on this farm he had some ducks
EIEIO
With a quack, quack, here and a quack, quack there
Here a quack
There a quack
Everywhere a quack, quack

Old Macdonald had a farm
EIEIO
And on this farm he had some pigs
EIEIO
With a oink, oink, here and a oink, oink there
Here a oink
There a oink
Everywhere a oink, oink

BARNEY IS SOOO BIG

21

Barney is so-o-o big. He can make a yummy sandwich.

24

Barney is so-o-o big.
He can play lots of music.

26

Barney is so-o-o big.
He can build a giant sand castle.

And I can make it pretty!

How big is Barney?
Barney is so-o-o big!
But I'm big, too.
And I'm getting bigger
every day!

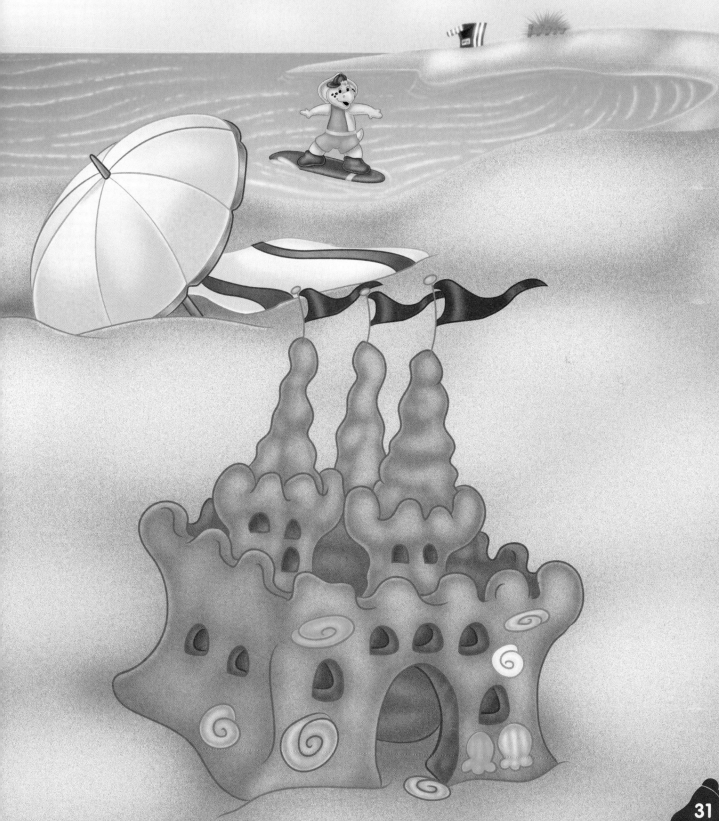

31

Alphabet colouring story

ABC
ABC
Do you know
Your ABC?
You can learn how to read today
Use your alphabet right away
If you look and then you say
Your ABC

1-2-3
1-2-3
Do you know
Your 1-2-3
You can learn how to count today
Use your numbering right away
If you look and then you say
Your 1-2-3

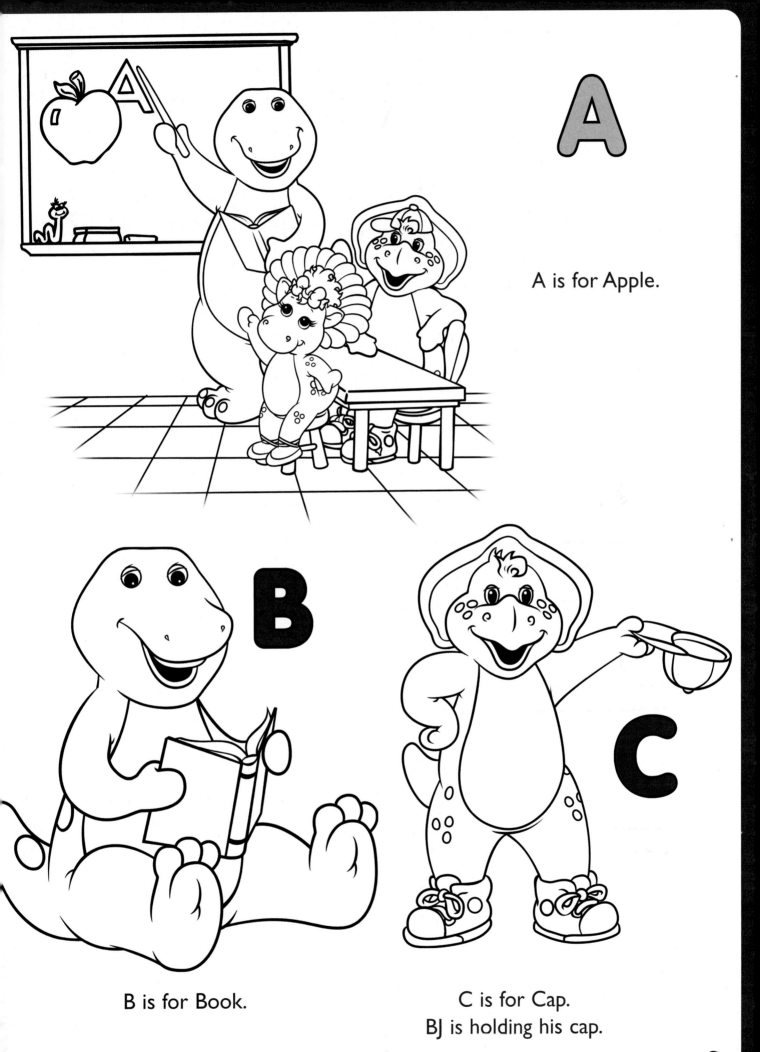

A

A is for Apple.

B

B is for Book.

C

C is for Cap.
BJ is holding his cap.

D

D is for Drum.
BJ and Barney play the drum's.

E is for Elephant.
Elephants are enormous.

E

F

F is for Flowers.
Fresh flowers smell good!

G

G is for Grapes.

H

H is for Hopscotch.
Baby Bop and BJ play hopscotch.

I

I is for Ice Cream.

J

J is for Jump.
Baby Bop jumps rope.

K is for Kite.
Kites fly high in the sky. **K**

L

L is for Leaves.

M

M is for Milk.
Milk keeps Baby Bop healthy.

N

N is for Nest.
Connect the dots to see
what's inside the Nest.

O is for Owl.

O

P

P is for Piano.
Barney plays the piano.

Q is for Queen.
Baby Bop pretends to be a queen.

R is for Rabbit.
Barney pets the rabbit.

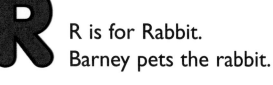

S is for Slide.

T

T is for Tricycle.
Baby Bop rides her tricycle.

U

U is for Umbrella.
Barney and BJ are
under the umbrellas.

V

V is for Volleyball.
Volleyball is fun
to play with friends.

W

W is for Winter.

X

X is for Xylophone.

Y

Y is for Yawn.

Z

Z is for Zebra.

Barney's Big Book of Manners

Somebody has sent Barney a parcel in the post.
"It's my friend Mary Smart's new book!" he smiles.
"Mary Smart's Book of Manners for Children!"

Mary Smart has invited Barney and his friends to a party!
"We will have to be on our best behaviour," says Baby Bop.

Barney looks in the book.
"To show good manners every day,
greet your friends in a friendly way!" he reads.
"How do you do!" giggles Baby Bop to Whitney.

"What else does it say about friends?" asks BJ.
"'Co-operate' means 'getting along'.
Work together, and you can't go wrong!
Everything's more fun when you share it with friends!"
smiles Barney.

Baby Bop sneezes.
"Let's see what the book says about sneezes," says Barney.
"Cover your mouth whatever you do, so others don't get sneezes too!"
"That's a good idea!" says Baby Bop. "ACHOOO!"

"We'd better get ready for the party!" says Barney.
"The book says: When you go to parties and other places,
it's important to show clean hands and faces!"

47

Everyone runs to wash their hands and faces.
They all want to be first!
Barney reads the next rule:
"When one thing is wanted by two or more,
that's what 'taking turns' is for!"

"We know a song about taking turns!"
says Barney.

Oh we take turns
When we play with toys
'cause that's what's right
For girls and boys!

Oh we take turns
When we play a game
'cause that's a rule
That stays the same!

Oh we take turns
So we'll all have fun
And we include
EVERYONE!

"Now, is everyone ready for the party?"
smiles Barney."Then let's go!"

Whiz! Whirr! Help Baby Bop and BJ find their way through Professor Tinkerputt's toy factory so everyone can play together!

Toy Factory Fun

Well done! Now go back to the beginning and play all over again!

Manners Matter

It was almost time for the party at Mary Smart's house. Barney and his friends all felt very excited. When they saw the house, they were amazed.

"It's a mansion!" exclaimed BJ.

"It's very, very big!" Baby Bop gasped.

Barney said that Nick could ring the doorbell. When he pressed it, there was a very long, loud burst of music. Everyone giggled!

"Now that's what I call a doorbell!" laughed BJ.

While the children were still giggling, the big door swung open and they saw a tall man in a black suit.

"Good afternoon," said the man, importantly. "Please step inside."

Barney and his friends entered and found themselves in a big hall, with marble floors and tinkling chandeliers.

"I am Miss Smart's butler, Baxter," said Baxter.

"I'm Barney and these are my friends," said Barney.

"Please wait here while I announce you to Miss Smart." Baxter replied.

Then he walked slowly away down a long corridor.

"This place is awesome!" shouted BJ.
He was so loud that his voice echoed
around the hall and rattled the chandeliers.
"BJ, you are too LOUD!" Baby Bop shouted. She made
the chandeliers rattle too!
"Before we get to the party," chuckled Barney, "I think we
need to practice another rule for good manners...!"
"What is it, Barney?" Gianna asked.
"Did you know you each have two voices?" said Barney.
Everyone looked surprised and shook their heads.

"You have an indoor voice and an outdoor voice!" Barney explained. "Your indoor voice is small and quiet, for when you're at home or at school. Your outdoor voice is BIG and STRONG and LOUD! You use it when you're playing outside! You have to be careful not to get them mixed up! Shall we practice?"

Everyone thought that sounded like lots of fun! They opened the front door. Barney went outside with Mario, BJ and Whitney. Baby Bop stayed in the hall with Nick, Gianna and Beth. They all practiced their indoor and outdoor voices – it got very noisy!

Barney and his friends were having so much fun that they didn't notice Baxter had come back. He didn't look amused!

"Miss Smart will see you now," Baxter frowned.

"Oops! I think we made too much noise!" said Beth.

They followed Baxter down the long, long corridor.

"Try not to make noise! Try not to make noise!" BJ kept telling himself.

At last they came to a big dark door. Baxter swung the door open and everyone gasped…

Mary Smart was standing in the middle of the room, surrounded by decorations and party games and lots of people having fun!

"Hello Barney!" she said. "It's wonderful to see you!"

"Mary," said Barney, "I'd like you to meet Whitney, Nick, Beth, Mario, Gianna, BJ and Baby Bop."

Mary Smart shook hands with everyone in turn.

"It's very nice to meet you!" said Baby Bop.

"Thank you! What good manners you have!" Mary smiled.

"We've been reading your new book of manners – it's stuuuuPENDous!" said Barney.

"I'm so glad you liked it!" Mary replied. "Now, I hope you're ready to have some fun?"

The children cheered, then remembered their manners just in time! "Yes please!"

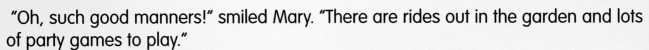

"Oh, such good manners!" smiled Mary. "There are rides out in the garden and lots of party games to play."

BJ, Baby Bop and the children ran off to find the party games.

"I'd like to try some of the games too," Barney said. "Would you care to join me?"

"I'd be delighted, thank you," said Mary. "I'll race you to the ring toss!"

"I just love parties!" chuckled Barney.

Everyone had lots of fun playing games and going on rides! Gianna and Nick tried the coconut shy first. Mario and Whitney went on the dodgems. Best of all, everyone remembered the things they had learned from the book of manners.
They all helped each other and shared, and that made the party even more fun! BJ and Baby Bop took turns at the ring toss. They enjoyed blowing their party horns as loud as they could!

At last everyone came back to tell Barney and Mary what they had been doing.

"Barney! Did you see me riding the pony?" asked Whitney.

"Yes, I did!" Barney chuckled. "You looked like a real cowgirl!"

"I threw the basketball in the hoop three times!" exclaimed Nick.

"That's wonderful!" Mary laughed.

"I went round and round on the merry-go-round!" said Gianna.

"A real parrot sat on my shoulder!" said Mario.

"I bounced way up high on the trampoline!" giggled Beth.

"This party's a blast!" BJ grinned.

"After all that running around, you must be hungry!" said Mary. "The goodies are right over here!"
She led them over to an enormous table. It was piled high with wonderful things to eat. Cakes and cookies! Pies and sweets! Cupcakes and fruit! There was even a punch bowl fountain! Everyone gasped in delight.

"Wow!" BJ exclaimed. "Let me at it!"
He grabbed a plate and reached out for a cookie.
"BJ," said Barney. "Before you serve yourself, you need to know the magic words!"
"I knew there was a catch," sighed BJ.
"Don't worry, BJ," Mary said with a big smile. "I'll be happy to tell you what the magic words are!"

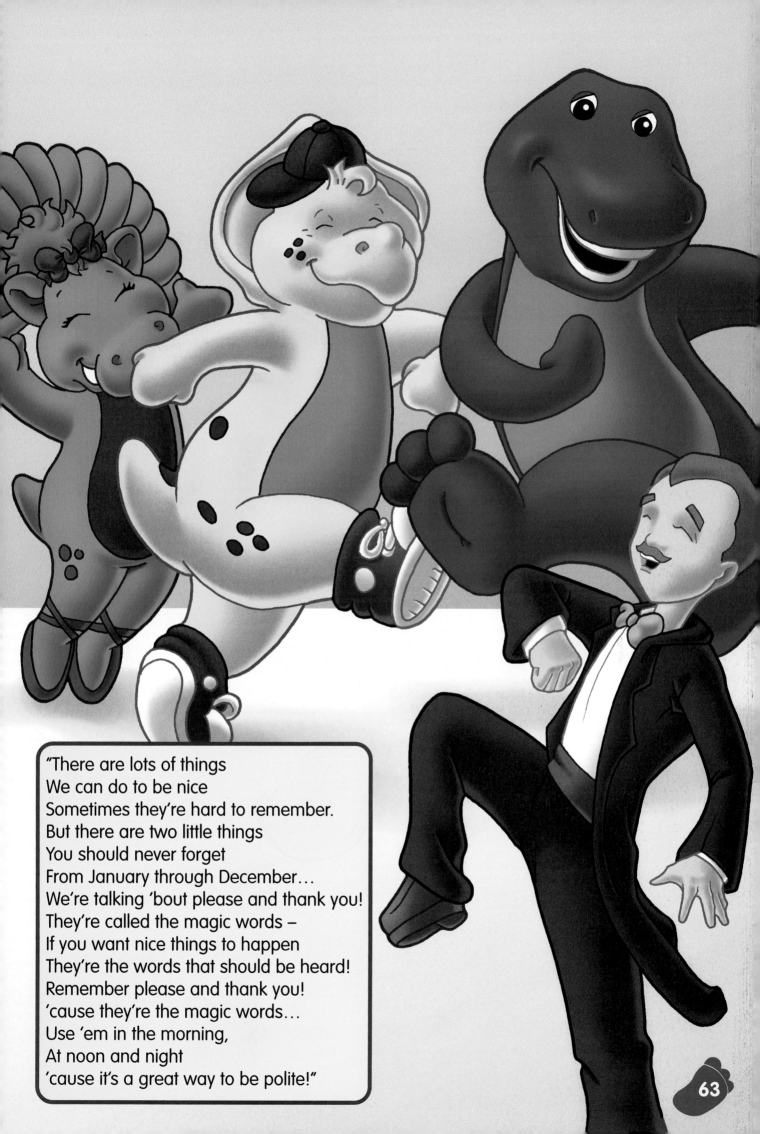

"There are lots of things
We can do to be nice
Sometimes they're hard to remember.
But there are two little things
You should never forget
From January through December…
We're talking 'bout please and thank you!
They're called the magic words –
If you want nice things to happen
They're the words that should be heard!
Remember please and thank you!
'cause they're the magic words…
Use 'em in the morning,
At noon and night
'cause it's a great way to be polite!"

Even Baxter joined in the song!
When they had finished singing, everyone helped themselves to something to eat.
They all remembered to say 'please' and 'thank you'!
Very soon all the food had gone.
"Did everyone get enough to eat?" asked Mary.
"I don't think I could eat anything else!" Gianna replied.
"I don't think I can even move!" groaned Mario.
"The pie was absolutely deeelicious!" said Barney.
"I liked the cupcakes and the cheese and crackers and the strawberries best!" giggled Baby Bop.
"This party's great," said BJ, patting his tummy happily.

"I'm glad you're enjoying it, BJ," smiled Mary.

"I'm really surprised," said BJ. "I didn't think you could have a great party when you need to use good manners!"

Everyone looked shocked!

"You didn't?" Mary exclaimed. "BJ, I don't think you finished reading my book!" She handed a copy of the book to Barney.

"Barney, would you please read the last rule in the book to BJ?"

"Yes I will!" Barney said with a big smile. "I think it's a very important rule for all my friends to know… it's FUN to use good manners!"

"That's what I was trying to say!" grinned BJ.

65

"And now I think it would show very good manners if we all had lots more fun!" said Mary. "What do you say?"
"Yes please!" everyone cheered.
"This party is the best!" Whitney smiled.
"I think BJ learned a lot about good manners today!" said Beth.
"I think we all did," said Mario.

"I'm very glad," chuckled Barney, "because using good manners is a very special way of being nice to other people, and letting them know that you really care – the way I care for all my friends!"
The children gave Barney a big hug.
"We care about you too, Barney!"

Can you see the deer?

Forgot your backpack? Go back 1 space

Backpacks are heavy. Take a break and skip a turn

Time for a picnic lunch. Go forward 1 space

Happy trails to you! Jump forward 1 space.

Back on ...ck. Lets hit the trail.

A raccoon stole my sandwich.

A swimming hole! Last one in is an unhappy camper. Jump ahead 1 space

Watch out for the waterfall! Go back 2 spaces.

Can you canoe? pretend you're rowing a boat!

Can you count the forest animals in this game?

Sing "Row, Row, Row Your Boat"

Barney says "Please"

"We're going to have a party," says Baby Bop.
"It's Mr. Bear's make-believe birthday!"

70

"Oh, a party sounds like fun," says Barney.
"And we can practice using good manners."

"What are manners?" Baby Bop asks.
"Manners are special ways to be nice
to other people," Barney tells her.

"One way to showgood manners is to say
'please' and 'thank you,'" Barney says.

"Let's try now," Barney says happily.
"Baby Bop, will you get some party dishes... please?"

Baby Bop brings lot of party dishes.
Barney says, "Thank you, Baby Bop."

Baby Bop says, "Barney, will you blow up
some party balloons...please?"

"I'll be happy to," answers Barney.
Barney blows up all the balloons.
Baby Bop says, "Thank you, Barney."

"Now let's make party snacks for Mr. Bear," says Barney.
"Baby Bop, will you get the peanut butter...please?"

"Yes, I will," laughs Baby Bop.
Baby Bop gets a big jar of peanut butter.

**Baby Bop and Barney take turns making
yummy sandwiches.
Barney says, "May I eat my sandwich now...please?"**

Baby Bop says, "Yes, you may."
Barney doesn't say anything after that...
because his mouth is full!
But after he chews and swallows, he says,
"Thank you, Baby Bop."

"Mr. Bear would like some party music,"
says Baby Bop.
"Barney, will you make some music...please?"

"Yes, I will," laughs Barney.
Barney makes lots of happy music. Crash-bang-boom!
Baby Bop says, "Thank you, Barney."

83

Barney says, "Baby Bop, would you put on a puppet show for Mr. Bear...please?"

**Barney claps his hands for Baby Bop's
wonderful puppet show.
Barney says, "Thank you, Baby Bop."**

"Now Mr. Bear wants to take a train ride," says Baby Bop. "Barney, will you drive the train...please?"

"Here we go," Barney laughs,
"Chugga-chugga, woo-woooo!"
Baby Bop says "Thank you, Barney."

When the train stops, Baby Bop puts her toys away.
"I hope you had fun at your party," Baby Bop says to Mr. Bear.
"Barney, will you help me clean the party dishes...please?"

"Of course I will," says Barney.
Baby Bop says, "Thank you, Barney."

**The two friends take turns washing and drying dishes.
Barney says, "Thank you for inviting
me to your nice party, Baby Bop."
Baby Bop smiles happily. "You're welcome," she says.**

Barney, BJ and Baby Bop are spending the day at the zoo. Their first stop is to see the tropical birds.

"BJ got a cracker?" squawks a funny voice in a tree.
"Look BJ!" cries Barney. "A toucan is talking to you!"
How many toucans can you find?

93

"I think the reptiles are my favourite zoo friends!" says BJ.
"Lizards, alligators and snakes, oh my!" cries Barney.

How many lizards can you find?

answer: 5

"I want to see the monkeys!" says BJ.
Baby Bop cries, "me too! Me too!"
"Look!" adds Barney. "Monkeys see, monkeys do!"

How many brown monkeys can you see?

"We're off to see the zebras, giraffes
and elephants!" calls Barney.

"Look at those elephants!" adds Baby Bop.
"They must eat a lot of peanuts to get so big!"
How many elephants can you find?

answer: 4

"I think I hear something!"
says Baby Bop. "Listen!"
"Roarrr!" growled a lion.

"That's what you call a rip-roaring roar," chuckles Barney.
"We had better not keep those lions and tigers waiting!"
How many cubs can you see?

answer: 4

"I'm hot," says Baby Bop.
"Where can we go to cool off?"
"Our last stop is the perfect place to
chill out," replies Barney.
"Follow me to Penguin Palace!"

102

"Cool!" cries BJ. "We have made
lots of new friends today."
"That's right," laughs Barney.
"Now we've got old friends,
new friends and zoo friends!"

103

The Wheels On Barney's Bus

The wheels on the bus go round and round,
Round and round, round and round.
The wheels on the bus go round and round,
All through the town!

The door on the bus goes open and shut,
Open and shut, open and shut.
The door on the bus goes open and shut,
All through the town.

The driver on the bus says, "Move back, please!"
"Move back, please! Move back, please!"
The driver on the bus says, "Move back, please!"
All through the town.

The wipers on the bus go swish, swish, swish!
Swish, swish, swish. Swish, swish, swish!
The wipers on the bus go swish, swish, swish!
All through the town.

The babies on the bus say, "Wah, wah, wah!"
"Wah, wah, wah! Wah, wah, wah!"
The babies on the bus say, "Wah, wah, wah!"
All through the town.

The mummy's on the bus say, "I love you!"
"I love you. I love you."
The mummy's on the bus say, "I love you!"
All through the town!

Astronaut Barney requests permission to come aboard.

One small step for Baby Bop.

3-2-1 - Blastoff!
Can you help guide
Barney's rocket ship
back to Earth?

Outer Space Adventure

Mr. Sun shines on.

This planet is out of this world!

...nee! It's first-class space cadet BJ!

There's no place like Earth!